Two Animal Tales from Africa

Written by Beverley Birch

Illustrated by Daniele Fabbri

Contents

Collins

The water thief

In the wide, hot plains of Africa, it hadn't rained for months.
The earth was thirsty. Trees and plants were thirsty, lakes and
river beds dry, cracked mud.

Animals, large and small, searched everywhere for water.
But water holes were dusty bowls in sun-baked ground.

Everyone feared they'd die of thirst.

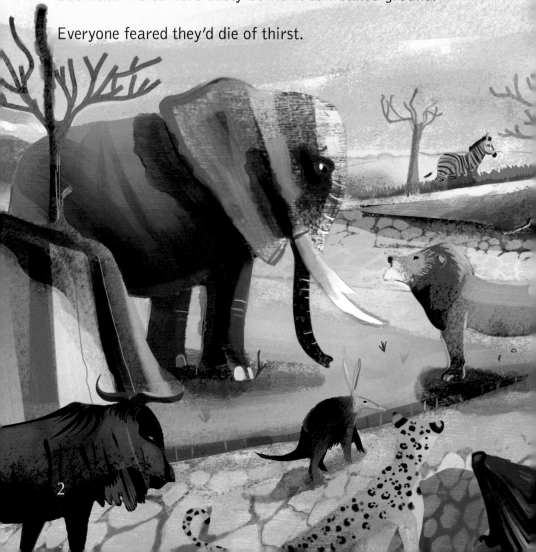

Elephant, who had a long memory, was remembering a place
in the forest where a river once tumbled across stones.
No river now, but last week he'd seen the trees were still green
and bushes grew, while everywhere else was withered, brown.

"These trees have sent roots deep into the earth and found
water," he told the other animals. "If we dig there, we'll find
water too, deep underground!"

Lion nodded his great maned head. "Worth a try, Elephant!"

So Elephant led them to the green place – Lion, Leopard, Hyena, Jackal, Monkey, Baboon, Squirrel, Warthog, Wildebeest, Zebra, Porcupine, even little Tortoise, trailing behind – all bringing their digging sticks. Except for Aardvark, whose long claws were perfect for digging.

All day they dug. Sun burnt down. It was thirsty work, and still no water. They went on into the night, and the next day again, thirstier than ever.

But they trusted Elephant, for he was wise.

Everyone, that is, except Hyena. He stretched out beneath a shady tree and snoozed. If you looked closely, you'd see one eye sneak open to check how deep the hole was.

"That lazy good-for-nothing!" Wildebeest muttered.

"When water comes, he'll slink in and drink and leave none for us!" wailed Monkey.

"We'll stop him," snarled Leopard.

At last, deep in the hole, soil became damp. More digging, and it was wetter. Then pools of water seeped in and, suddenly, clear water gushed up from a spring running deep in the earth.

Joyfully, they carried slabs of rock to make stepping stones in the water hole, and each had a sip of life-giving water, and felt much better.

There might be enough here till the next rains came!

"We've worked hard to make this water hole," said Lion. "Only animals who've helped should drink." And he scowled at Hyena, who (of course) was wide awake the moment water appeared.

"Let's take turns to guard it," said Porcupine.

An excellent plan! Everyone dragged branches of thorn bush, piling them high to make a thick fence no animal could cross. They glared at Hyena.

Hyena just wandered away, laughing, as if he didn't have a care in the world.

He had a plan, too.

He fetched two bowls made from the fruit of baobab trees.
In one, he put a strong rope of twisted vines, and he hid this
bowl under a rock.

Then he took the other bowl to beehives full of rich honey,
sweet-smelling from the flowers the bees visited. He put some
honey in the bowl, and hid that under the rock, too.

He settled down to doze till nightfall.

Meanwhile, Wildebeest stood squarely by a tree, marking the only gap in the thorn-bush fence round the water hole. The sun fell behind the trees. He lowered his shaggy head and waggled his horns. "No thief will escape me!"

He spotted Hyena's yellow eyes shining through the dark; then Hyena himself strolling closer, carrying two bowls. He was sipping from them, licking his lips and rolling his eyes with delight.

"You lazy creature, keep away!" bellowed Wildebeest.
"Don't dare steal our water. I'll spear you with my horns!"

"Your water!" sneered Hyena. "Ugh! Full of mud from
your digging. Sour! Ugh! Ugh! Why drink that foul stuff?
Here's my own sweet water!" And he pretended to drink from
the honey bowl.

"Where did you get water?" Wildebeest demanded, suspiciously.

"From the sweetest spring," answered Hyena, taking
another "drink", and smacking his lips. He pretended
to think. "See here, Wildebeest, you're working away
there, I'll be kind and let you taste."

He picked a grass stalk, dipped it in the honey
bowl and gave it to Wildebeest.

Oh, the taste
and perfume of
forest flowers!
"Wonderful!"
cried Wildebeest.
"Oh, let me
drink again!"

11

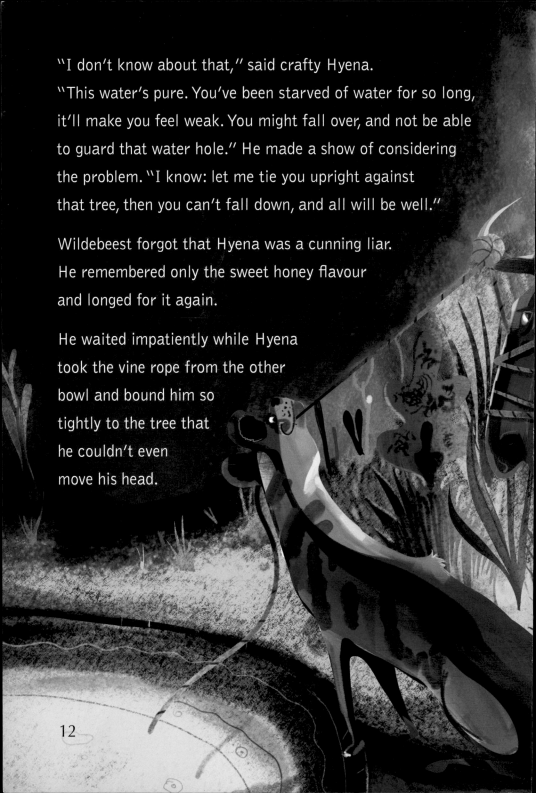

"I don't know about that," said crafty Hyena.
"This water's pure. You've been starved of water for so long,
it'll make you feel weak. You might fall over, and not be able
to guard that water hole." He made a show of considering
the problem. "I know: let me tie you upright against
that tree, then you can't fall down, and all will be well."

Wildebeest forgot that Hyena was a cunning liar.
He remembered only the sweet honey flavour
and longed for it again.

He waited impatiently while Hyena
took the vine rope from the other
bowl and bound him so
tightly to the tree that
he couldn't even
move his head.

13

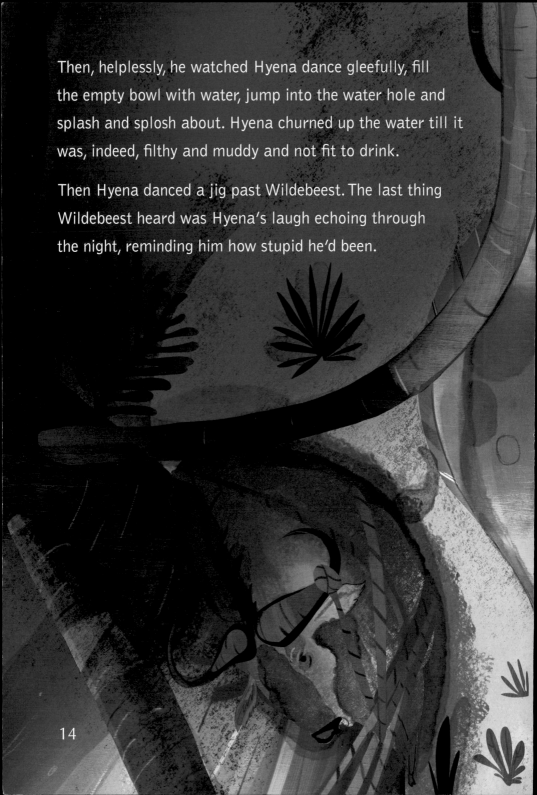

Then, helplessly, he watched Hyena dance gleefully, fill the empty bowl with water, jump into the water hole and splash and splosh about. Hyena churned up the water till it was, indeed, filthy and muddy and not fit to drink.

Then Hyena danced a jig past Wildebeest. The last thing Wildebeest heard was Hyena's laugh echoing through the night, reminding him how stupid he'd been.

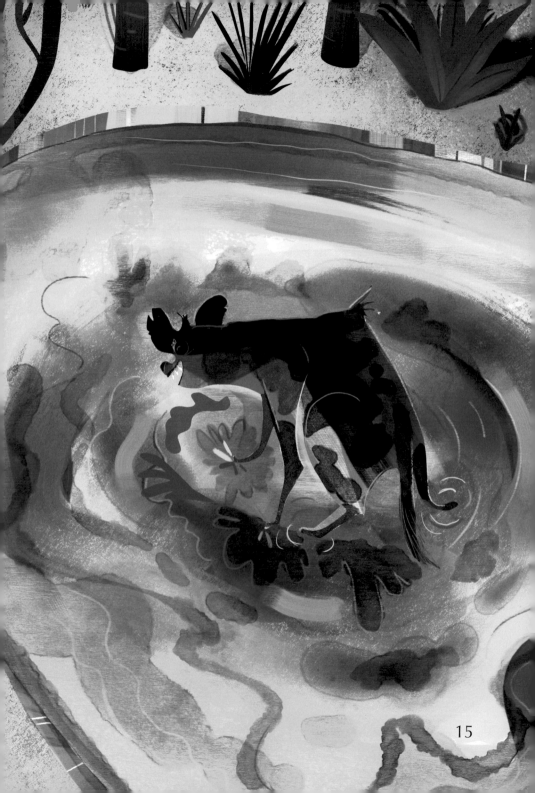

15

What shame! What to tell the others? He had the whole night to worry about it. By morning, he'd invented a very tall story.

"You should've seen this great gang of men with spears! I couldn't stop them! They tied me, and drank and washed in the water hole."

Tortoise watched Wildebeest closely, and wondered – but said nothing.

Lion growled. "No gang will dare challenge me!
Tonight, I'll defend our water!"

Sorry to say, though Lion was big and strong and fiercer
than most animals, he, too, gave in to curiosity and greed
when Hyena wandered by with his tale of sweet water.
Lion, too, ended up roped to that tree. And again, in
the morning, the water wasn't fit to drink.

"Oh, I tied myself," lied Lion. "I was afraid I'd fall
over asleep! But I did, and someone sneaked in."

Tortoise listened, and thought his thoughts, and said nothing.

17

Now, Elephant had a strong suspicion that none of this was true. Something's going on here, he thought, and I'll discover what! "My turn tonight," he declared.

You'd think Elephant, of all animals, would be clever enough not to be tricked, wouldn't you?

Sad to say, he just fell under the spell of that honey-taste and Hyena's trickery.

Now Tortoise spoke up, in his careful, slow way. "Let me catch this thief at our water hole."

"You!" everyone snorted. "Plodding along with your short legs and your heavy shell? You're much too slow!" They always laughed at Tortoise, especially when he sang his song:

I move house,
And I never move house.
I'm at home, wherever I go!

But Elephant knew well that not size, or strength or speed would stop this thief. He was bitterly guilty for letting himself be fooled. "Tortoise can't do worse than the rest of us," he said. And because Elephant always knew best, everyone agreed.

"First," said Tortoise, "find the tree with the stickiest sap. Then, smear the sap over my shell. Every bit of it. Then all go away and leave me alone."

20

Night fell. Tortoise crawled past the stepping stones into the shallows at the edge of the water hole. Only the top of his shell showed above water, shining in the moonlight as if it was the last stepping stone.

Along came Hyena. No one's keeping watch? "The water hole's mine! I've tricked them all!" he yelled. And to celebrate, he ate all the honey he had in his bowl.

"Now for a swim!" He trotted across the stones towards the water. He put a paw on the last stone. But, when he tried to lift it, he couldn't. He stood on the other paws, to help pull the stuck one off.

Now he had four paws he couldn't move. He yanked and yanked, but the more he struggled, the more glued he was. Exhausted, he sat down to think.

You can guess what else stuck fast then!

As the sun rose and everyone gathered for a morning drink, there was Tortoise plodding slowly along with Hyena in the middle of a very sticky problem not even he could squirm out of.

After that, no one said a single rude word about little Tortoise, ever again. What's more, they thought he was the cleverest of all the animals – even, some whispered, wiser than Elephant.

Lumbwi and the gazelle

Every day, Lumbwi searched rubbish dumps for food. On good days, he found some. It was sometimes too rotten to eat. Sometimes, he found something to sell for real food, but not often. He had nothing but his name, Lumbwi – meaning chameleon in Swahili and the hut he'd made from scraps of wood and card.

One day, however, he found a small coin, just enough to buy a spoon of soup. His mouth watered, imagining.

Just then, a man trundled a rickety cart along, carrying a cage of woven twigs. Inside were gazelles, scraggy loops of rope round their necks.

The littlest gazelle lifted its head and looked at Lumbwi with large, sad eyes. The thought floated into Lumbwi's head that a gazelle would be company. He held out the coin.

The gazelle man looked hard at the young man, and then at the gazelle. The coin wasn't enough even for the rope round the animal's neck, but he couldn't stop himself pulling the little gazelle from the cage and putting the rope into Lumbwi's hand.

For the first time ever, Lumbwi felt lucky. He led the gazelle home, tied it to a post near his hut, and tugged leaves from a bush nearby. Then he gazed at the graceful creature nibbling. He forgot his own hunger.

"Swala," he whispered — meaning gazelle in Swahili. Swala gazed back, chewing slowly.

Next day, Lumbwi rushed home and led Swala to find grass to graze. After that, he kept Swala close, and chatted to him.

Of course, Swala didn't answer. Until one day, as Lumbwi stirred soup boiled from vegetable peelings, a soft voice spoke. "Master."

He swung round. Only Swala was there, no one else.

Again. "Master. Hear me."

With a jolt of fear, Lumbwi understood.

"Master," repeated Swala, "I'm born to be free. I beg you, let me roam the plains, free. I'll return each night, always."

Lumbwi could only gasp, "How can you talk?"

"I reveal it to you, because I trust you."

All night, Lumbwi thought about this magical Swala. What if he doesn't come back? I'll be alone again. He shivered. But next morning, he took the rope off Swala's neck, and watched him leap into the bushes with a twitch of his black tail, as if he had wings.

All day, Lumbwi worried. As evening sun dipped towards the horizon, he hurried home. Swala was stepping daintily into his hut. After that, every dawn, Swala went. Every night, he returned.

Now, they had long conversations. Lumbwi told Swala of his loneliness before Swala came. Swala told Lumbwi about life on the open plains before hunters trapped him and caged him, and sold him to the gazelle man. He grew strong and healthy; his reddish coat and the black and white markings of his face became sleek and glossy.

One day, as he grazed in the midday heat, he glimpsed something glittering far off on the plain. He went closer. Cushioned in the grass, sunlight glancing off it like a flame, was an enormous diamond.

He was about to rush home and give it to Lumbwi – for a gazelle doesn't need a diamond. But Lumbwi will lose it to some dishonest person who gives him a coin, he thought. Lumbwi will be happy to have meals in his belly. He won't see the great wealth passing from him in the blink of an eye. Or he'll keep it because it's pretty, and someone will kill him for it.

He lay down in the shade of a rock to think. Before long, he had a plan: one that could bring Lumbwi fortune far beyond the value of any diamond.

I'll offer it to the sultan to show friendship from my master, a prince from over the sea. That'll please the sultan. People say he has enemies who want to be sultan instead, so he longs for friends, and is generous when he finds one.

At once, Swala set off for the sultan's palace, the diamond hidden in a bundle of leaves in his mouth.

The sultan sat below a yellow silk umbrella in his court, listening to reports from his ministers about his land. When the handsome gazelle laid the sparkling diamond before him, he was charmed.

He was even more enchanted when the fine animal began to talk of his wonderful master who offered friendship.

Any man who owns such a clever and loyal beast must be great indeed, he thought. "Your master must be my guest," he said. "I wish to thank him."

Swala's heart quickened with joy. Almost as fast as the wind, he raced to tell Lumbwi.

"Important men don't sent invitations to me! It must be a trick!" Lumbwi decided, suspiciously.

"Trust me, Master," pleaded Swala. "Haven't I kept my promise? I promise now, you'll be safe, and your life will be good ... Just pretend to be this prince, and let me do the talking."

And so Lumbwi set off to the sultan's palace with Swala.

By a river, Swala stopped. "The sultan must really think that you're the rich prince who sent him the diamond," he said. "He mustn't see your rags, or he won't believe us, and he always fears tricks from his enemies. Bury your clothes, and wash in the river. Then lie on the ground, as if you're hurt. It must look as if thieves took everything you own."

Lumbwi obediently fell down, and Swala bounded away to the sultan.

"Help! Robbers attacked the prince, my master, and stole everything!"

"Bring him here!" the sultan ordered servants. "Prepare water softened with oils and perfumes to soothe the prince's wounds!"

They bathed Lumbwi, and wrapped him in soft clothes. He lay on a red silk couch, staring at foods carried in to tempt him. Such food! Meats, vegetables, fruits, sweets of dates and honey, and goblets of golden juices. All for just one person? He was in a dream.

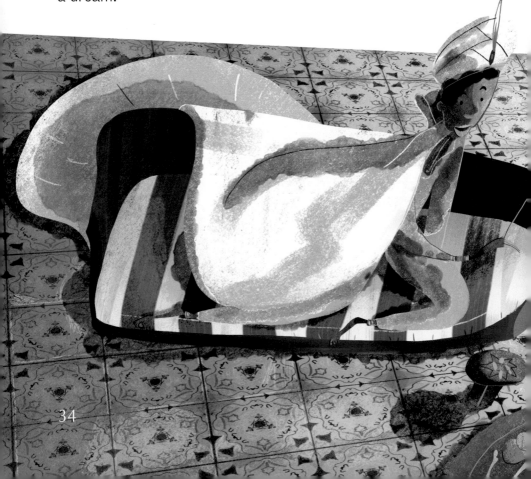

The poor prince! These evil men have left him dazed, decided the sultan. He said out loud, "My friend, rest here, till you're well again."

By next morning, Lumbwi had stopped feeling in a dream, or afraid he'd be found out. He was enjoying himself.

The truth is, this sultan was bored with people asking favours. Prince Lumbwi asked for nothing. He found delight in everything. He was never angry. The sultan liked that. His guest was also generous – after all, he'd given a diamond, and asked nothing in return. Everyone else wanted something.

Before long, the sultan and Lumbwi were firm friends. And, believing him to be such a good and generous man — and rich — the sultan was happy his own daughter thought Lumbwi was a handsome, pleasant young man. Within a month, the palace was decked with flags and silken canopies for Lumbwi's marriage to the sultan's daughter. Feasts and celebrations, music and dancing went on for days and nights.

How Swala rejoiced at Lumbwi, splendid in his silk robes and turban, beside the sultan's lovely daughter! Their wedding present from her father was a beautiful palace with fountains and gardens, balconies cooled by sea breezes, and servants to bring him and his young wife everything they needed.

Of course, Lumbwi was busy now. They couldn't chat the way they used to. But Swala understood.

"There's nothing more I can do," said Swala. "Now he owes me my freedom." He was a little upset, though, that Lumbwi agreed without even pausing, and rushed away to watch a display of juggling.

Yet Swala longed for freedom on the grasslands, far from towns and people.

This mood didn't last. He missed those times he and Lumbwi had shared their hopes and dreams with each other. From time to time, he went close to the palace, and left messages for Lumbwi that he was near, hoping.

Lumbwi sent no word back. Sadness settled on Swala. If I say I'm ill, my friend will rush to my side, he thought.

Lumbwi didn't. He sent food.

Swala stopped roaming the grasslands. He stopped eating, and became truly weak. Before long, a fever took hold ...

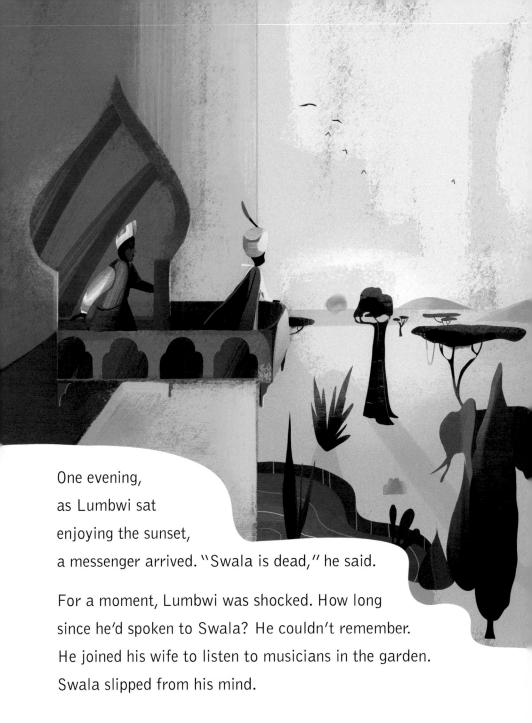

One evening,
as Lumbwi sat
enjoying the sunset,
a messenger arrived. "Swala is dead," he said.

For a moment, Lumbwi was shocked. How long
since he'd spoken to Swala? He couldn't remember.
He joined his wife to listen to musicians in the garden.
Swala slipped from his mind.

A few days later, the sultan said, "Swala must tell me of his travels."

"Oh, he's dead," said Lumbwi, not seeing the sultan's horror at how easily he said this.

"You didn't think to tell me, so I could honour him at burial?"

"Oh, I haven't buried him!" answered Lumbwi. "He's just an animal, and he only cost a coin."

The sultan turned abruptly and left the room. "I'm ashamed for your husband!" he told his daughter. "He's heartless. Swala should be buried with proper respect, to rest in peace!"

"I'm ashamed too," she told Lumbwi. "You didn't visit Swala. You disappoint me!"

"I don't have to do what you say!" Lumbwi replied, angrily.

So she too turned her back, too upset to say more, and in this mood, went to bed, leaving Lumbwi sitting grumpily.

"How dare they talk to me like that!" he muttered.
"I'm busy. I don't have time to chase after Swala. He's part
of the old life. I've got a new life now!" He sat up crossly,
grumbling, late into the night, and fell asleep on the couch.

In the night, his wife dreamt that Swala trotted elegantly through the palace, singing, and she was crying. When she woke, she was in her father's palace, in her old room before she married. Yet she knew she hadn't travelled.

"There's magic here," she whispered, "and it's that splendid Swala's magic. He's saying farewell through my dream."

Lumbwi began to dream, too. In the dream, he was lying on bare, beaten earth. No couch, no silks or cushions. Just his rickety old hut, and embers of his old fire, and his ragged old clothes on his back, the ones Swala had told him to bury by the river.

When he woke, it was no longer just a dream. It was true.

And now there was no longer Swala to make his life happier. Each day was as it was before Swala. Lumbwi hadn't learnt true, unselfish friendship, or not to betray it. So now Lumbwi was alone again, and had nothing.

45

A story of friendship

What Swala does for Lumbwi

What Lumbwi does for Swala

Ideas for reading

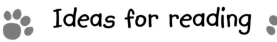

Written by Clare Dowdall, PhD
Lecturer and Primary Literacy Consultant

Reading objectives:
- increase familiarity with a wide range of books including fairy stories and retell orally
- ask questions to improve understanding
- identify main ideas drawn from more than one paragraph and summarise ideas

Spoken language objectives:
- participate in discussions, presentations, performances, role play, improvisations and debates

Curriculum links: Geography – locational knowledge, Africa; PSHE – health and well-being

Resources: art materials for mask making; music to accompany story telling

Build a context for reading

- Ask children to find the continent of Africa on a world map. Share what is known about the animals of Africa.
- Look at the image on the front cover and identify as many animals as possible. Discuss who preys on who, and who might be the cleverest.
- Read the blurb to the children. Discuss what the adjective "crafty" means, and what children know about hyenas and their characteristics.

Understand and apply reading strategies

- Read the title *The water thief* together, then read to p3. Ask children to suggest why water is going to be important in this story.